A NOTE TO PARENTS

Young children can be overwhelmed by their emotions--often because they don't understand and can't express what they are feeling. This, in turn, can frustrate parents. How can you help your child deal with a problem if the two of you don't even share a common vocabulary?

Welcome to **HOW I FEEL**--a series of books designed to bridge this communication gap. With simple text, lively illustrations, and an interactive format, each book describes familiar situations to help children recognize a particular emotion. It gives them a vocabulary to talk about what they're feeling, and it offers practical suggestions for dealing with those feelings.

Each time you read this book with your child you can reinforce the message with one of the following activities:

- Ask your child to make up a story about a little boy or girl who is afraid.

- Make a list together of words--real or imaginary--that mean "scared."

- Act out situations that spark your child's fear.

- Explore different degrees of fear with the Sizing-Up-Fear activity card and reusable stickers included with this book.

I hope you both enjoy the **HOW I FEEL** series, and that it will help your child take the first steps toward understanding emotions.

Marcia Leonard

Executive Producers, JOHN CHRISTIANSON and RON BERRY
Art Design, GARY CURRANT
Layout Design, CURRANT DESIGN GROUP and BEST IMPRESSION GRAPHICS

All rights reserved.
Text copyright ©1998,1999 MARCIA LEONARD
Illustrations copyright ©1998,1999 CHRIS SHARP
© SMART KIDS PUBLISHING, INC.
Published by PENTON OVERSEAS, INC.
No part of this book may be reproduced, copied or utilized in any form or manner
without written permission from the publisher. For information write to:
PENTON OVERSEAS, INC. • 2470 Impala Drive, Carlsbad, CA 92008-7226
(800) 748-5804

HOW I FEEL

SCARED

by Marcia Leonard
illustrated by Bartholomew

This little girl doesn't like the dark.
She feels scared.

This little boy is scared, too.
There's a bug crawling on his arm.

These kids are afraid of the neighbor's dog.

Would he scare you, too?
Can you make a face that looks scared?

This little girl is scared of thunder,
but her big sister likes it.

Do loud noises frighten you?

This little boy climbed up high.
Now he's afraid to climb down.

Has that ever happened to you?
What would you do?

It's okay to be scared.
That scary feeling is your body's way
of telling you to be careful.

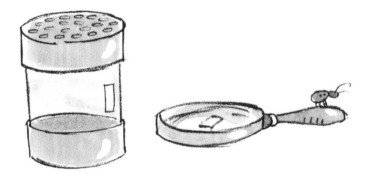

Sometimes it helps to learn about
what scares you.

Sometimes you can get used to it--
a little at a time.

And sometimes you can even
make friends with what scares you!

The most important thing
is to tell Mommy or Daddy
when you are scared,
because they can help you
make the scared feeling go away.

SIZING-UP-FEAR
Instructions

Use this Sizing-Up-Fear chart to help your child express the intensity of a particular fear. Gently remove the page of reusable stickers from the center of this book. Ask your child to choose one of the stickers representing typical childhood fears and place it in the *Fear* column. Then help your child use the colored stickers to cover up the girl or boy figure a little or a lot, depending on the size of his or her fear. How does your child feel about thunder and lightning? Is it only a tiny bit scary? Cover the figure's feet. Is it extremely scary? Cover the whole body. Try this with other fear stickers. Talk about the size of different fears--and ways to make them smaller.